The Snow Lambs

Debi Gliori

SCHOLASTIC PRESS
New York

For my good friends,
Johnnie, Mary, Rosie, and Sam

Copyright © 1995 by Debi Gliori.

All rights reserved. Published by Scholastic Press,
a division of Scholastic Inc., *publishers since 1920.*
555 Broadway, New York, NY 10012, by arrangement with
Scholastic Children's Books, Scholastic Publications Ltd.

No part of this publication may be reproduced in whole or in part, or stored
in a retrieval system, or transmitted in any form, or by any means, electronic,
mechanical, photocopying, recording, or otherwise, without written permission
of the publisher. For information regarding permission, write
to Scholastic Children's Books, Scholastic Publications Ltd., Commonwealth House, 1-19
New Oxford Street, London WC1A 1NU, England.

Library of Congress Cataloging-in-Publication Data

Gliori, Debi.
The snow lambs / by Debi Gliori.
p.   cm.
Summary: Because she is on a rescue mission, Bess, the sheep dog, fails to respond
when Sam's dad calls her to return home as a winter storm approaches.
ISBN 0-590-20304-5
[1. Sheep dogs—Fiction. 2. Snow—Fiction. 3. Storms—Fiction.]
I. Title. PZ7.G4889Sp 1996
[E]—dc20   95-25978
CIP
AC
12 11 10 9 8 7 6 5 4 3 2 1   6 7 8 9/9 0 1/0

Printed in Singapore   46

First American printing, October 1996

The artwork for this book was prepared in watercolor.
The text was set in New Caledonia semi-bold.

It was just before supper when the snow started falling. Sam, his dad, and Bess the sheepdog were counting in the sheep from the field.

"I think you counted that sheep twice, Dad," said Sam.
Dad was looking up at the sky where storm clouds gathered.
The branches on the old elm creaked, and Sam shivered.
He looked around. *I wonder where Bess is*, he thought.
"If the wind picks up, that old elm could blow down across
the power lines, and we'd be in trouble," said Dad.

Mom wrapped Sam up in a warm towel and dried his hair.

"That's quite a storm brewing out there," said Mom.

"Will Bess be blown away?" asked Sam.

"Don't worry, Sam. Bess can look after herself," she said.

The wind felt full of sharp little teeth,
nibbling at Sam's nose and biting his ears.

"Come on, Sam, let's get these sheep in,"
said Dad.

"I can't see Bess anywhere," said Sam.
"Where is she?"

When the sheep were safe inside,
Dad yelled, "BESS! BESS! COME HERE!"

His voice was lost in the wind.
"Come on, Sam, let's get you inside —
you look half frozen," he said.

They took off their boots and coats in the mud room. Dad bolted the door behind them.

"But how will Bess get in?" asked Sam.

"She won't," said Dad. "That dog is useless. Maybe being shut out will teach her a lesson."

After supper it was bathtime. Sam jumped into his bath with a huge SPLASH. *Bess will need a good hot bath when she comes home*, he thought.

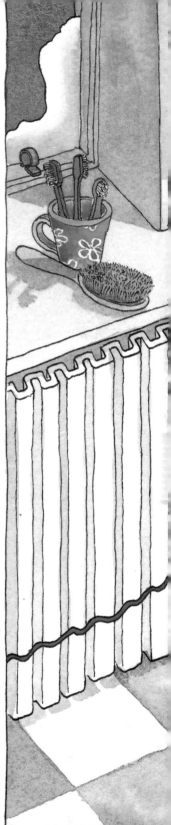

I hope Bess doesn't have to dig her way home,
thought Sam, digging out his pajamas.

Sam wriggled into his pajamas.
HELP! he thought. *I can't see a thing.*
Outside, snow filled the sky with blinding white flakes.
I hope Bess can see to find her way home, thought Sam.

Sam asked Dad to read him a monster story,
and then wished he hadn't. It was a very scary story.
Outside, the wind howled.

"I hope Bess isn't scared, too," whispered Sam.

The wind grew louder, hurling itself at the house as if it wanted to tear the roof off.

"Bed's the safest place on a night like this," said Dad.

"No!" said Sam.

"Come on, Sam. Upstairs," said Mom.

"I'm not going," cried Sam.
"I've got to wait up for Bess."

"It's all right, Sam," said Mom. "It's only a power outage."

"I knew it," said Dad. "That old elm has brought down the power lines."

"Oh, poor Bess!" said Sam. "How will she find our house when there are no lights?"

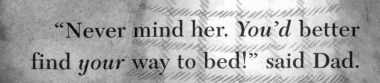

"Never mind her. *You'd* better
find *your* way to bed!" said Dad.

But Sam couldn't sleep.
He kept thinking about Bess.

He could hear something outside,
over the howl of the wind.

It sounded like a sheep bleating.
Sam tiptoed downstairs...

... and unbolted the door.
At first Sam could see nothing
through the whirling snowflakes.

Then something large and wet blundered past him, followed by Bess ... BESS!

"You're covering me in mud, Bess!" laughed Sam. Then he looked around and thought, *Uh-oh!* He rushed upstairs to get Mom and Dad.

"Well, Bess, it looks like you're a better shepherd than I am," said Dad. "What a clever dog to bring my best ewe home to lamb!"

Sam wrapped his arms tightly around Bess and whispered in her ear, "Brave Bess, I knew what a clever dog you were all along. I'm so glad you're home."

And later, when the wind had dropped
from a howl to a whisper, the kitchen
filled with newborn bleating.

"They're snow lambs!" said Sam.
It was the perfect place to be born.

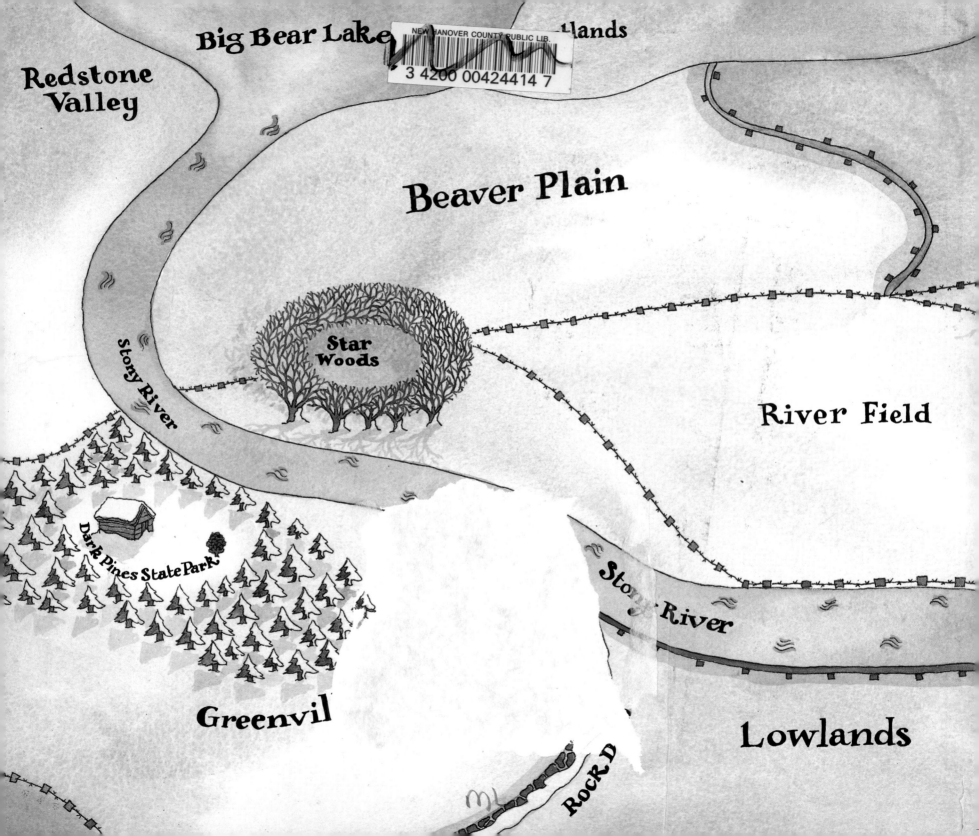